Green Earrings

and a

Felt Hat

Written by Jerry Newman

drawings by Margaret Hewitt

Henry Holt and Company ◆ New York

For Zoë, with apologies for all the times I neglected
to notice your earrings, and for Zoë and Vanessa, Rafaël and
Caroline, and Adam and Maggie
—J.N.

For William
—M.H.

Text copyright © 1993 by Jerry Newman
Illustrations copyright © 1993 by Margaret Hewitt
Published by Henry Holt and Company, Inc.,
115 West 18th Street, New York, New York 10011.
Published simultaneously in Canada by Fitzhenry & Whiteside Ltd.,
91 Granton Drive, Richmond Hill, Ontario L4B 2N5.
First edition

Library of Congress Cataloging-in-Publication Data
Newman, Jerry.
Green earrings and a felt hat/Jerry Newman; illustrations by Margaret Hewitt.
Summary: Two best friends have a disagreement and after returning each other's
borrowed possessions, they discover that it is their friendship they miss the most.
ISBN 0-8050-2392-5 (alk. paper)
[1. Friendship— Fiction.] I. Hewitt, Margaret, ill. II. Title.
PZ7.N47985G1 1993 [Fic]— dc20 92-29056

Printed in the United States of America
on acid-free paper. ∞

1 3 5 7 9 10 8 6 4 2

Green Earrings and a Felt Hat

Susan and Carolyn were the best of
friends.

They were such good friends, in fact, that they were always trading things back and forth. If Susan had something that Carolyn liked, she would lend it to her, and Carolyn would do the same. They traded so many things that sometimes they forgot who had what. They saw each other or spoke with each other every day, and often their conversations sounded like this:

"I can't find my green earrings," Susan would say.

"*I've* got your green earrings," Carolyn would answer. "I can't find my felt hat."

"*I've* got your felt hat," Susan would say.

It got so that each of them knew exactly what the other one was missing before she said it.

"In case you're looking for your green earrings," Carolyn would say, "I've got them."

"And in case you're looking for your felt hat," Susan would answer, "I've got it."

"And I've got your *Wind in the Willows*!"

"I've got your *Peter Pan*!"

"And I've got your orange Frisbee!"

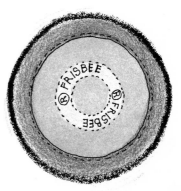

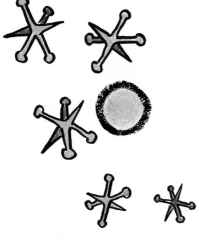

"I've got your set of jacks!"

"And I've got your polka-dot shirt!"

But underneath all of this what each
of them was thinking was, *I've got you
as my best friend, and I'm so glad!*
Carolyn liked Susan so much it
didn't seem possible to her that Susan

liked her just as much. Sometimes
she worried that Susan would rather
be best friends with Jenny or Emily or
one of the other girls in their class.
Susan liked Carolyn so much it didn't
seem possible to her that Carolyn
liked her just as much. Sometimes
she worried that Carolyn would rather
be best friends with Vivian or Krishna
or one of the other girls in their class.

One day they were over
at Carolyn's house doing
one of the things
they liked best,
which was to
listen to each
other's favorite
music.

Carolyn had just bought a new
cassette with some money she'd saved
from her last birthday, and was excited
about playing it for Susan. They lis-
tened to it and Susan agreed that it
was great.

Then she brought out a
new cassette that she had
gotten for her birthday
and that she couldn't
wait to play for Carolyn.
But before Carolyn
could listen to
it she said,

"Do you mind if we listen to my tape
again?"

Susan agreed. But then when Carolyn asked if they could play it again, for a *third* time, Susan began to get mad.

"Aren't we ever going to listen to *mine*?"

"Well, of course we are," said Carolyn. "But don't you just love mine? Vivian got the same one for her birthday and she says it's her favorite!"

"Well," Susan answered. "Emily told me she can't wait to hear *my* tape. She heard a bit of it on the radio and she says she thinks it's *the best one ever made*!"

This was true enough, but Susan had said it just to get back at Carolyn for mentioning Vivian.

"Well, if that's how you feel," said Carolyn. "Maybe you should take your tape over to Emily's house and play it for her."

Then they got so mad at each other that—

"You might as well take back your green earrings," Carolyn said. "I don't want them anymore!"

"And you might as well take back your felt hat!" said Susan.

"And you might as well take back your *Wind in the Willows*!"

"And you might as well take back your *Peter Pan!*"

"And you might as well take back your orange Frisbee!"

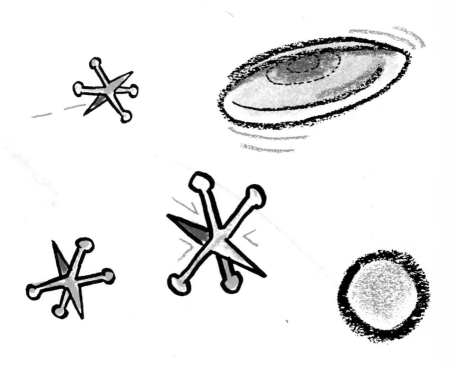

"And you might as well take back your set of jacks!"

"And you might as well take back your polka-dot shirt!"

But underneath all of this what each of them was thinking was, *This is terrible! I'm losing my best friend!*

Then for days and *days* they didn't speak to each other, and each of them grew more and more miserable. Carolyn began to walk to school with Vivian, who was lots of fun, and made her laugh, but it just wasn't the same. And she traded some of her favorite books with Krishna, who also loved to read. Krishna didn't like the same books she did, though, the way Susan always had.

At home, Carolyn would wander around looking for *The Wind in the Willows*, until she remembered it belonged to Susan, and she'd given it back to her. Even if she had her own copy, she thought, there was no one else in the entire world who loved it as much as she did, except for Susan.

Susan went down to the Tricks and Magic store that she and Carolyn used to go to almost every day. It wasn't nearly as much fun to go there alone, but she couldn't think of anyone else in the world she wanted to go there with.

Each of them spent long hours staring out the window of her bedroom, wondering what to do with herself and why she felt so sad much of the time. Carolyn was sure that by now Susan and Jenny were each other's best friend. Susan was sure that

Carolyn and Krishna were best friends, and that neither of them wanted to be friends with her. She thought that she would never have a best friend again.

Susan's mother noticed that something was the matter. "What's wrong, Susan?" she asked. But Susan just answered in a hopeless sort of voice, "Nothing, Mom. I'm *fine*."

"Did something happen between you and Carolyn? I haven't seen her around here in days."

"Oh, *her*," Susan said.

"And where's that poster of the movie star that you and Carolyn like so much?"

"Oh, *that*," said Susan.

She couldn't tell her mother that she'd had a stupid argument with her best friend and now they weren't speaking to each other. That was a secret, and the only person she could share a secret like that with was the very person she wasn't speaking with!

Carolyn's father noticed that something was the matter with Carolyn. "Is everything all right?" he asked.

But Carolyn just replied in a hopeless sort of voice, "Nothing, Dad. I'm *fine*."

"Did something happen between you and Susan? You two don't seem to be seeing as much of each other lately."

"Oh, *her*," Carolyn said.

"And where's that poster of the movie star that you and she like so much?"

"Oh, *that*," said Carolyn.

One day Susan
was looking for
something special
to wear and thought

of the felt hat. Then she remembered
that it belonged to Carolyn and she
had given it back to her.

She had hats of her
own, but none of them
looked half as good on
her. They were boring,
boring, *boring*.

She finally had to admit to herself that it wasn't the hat she really missed. It was Carolyn. It seemed life without her best friend just wasn't the same. There wasn't anyone—except Carolyn—she wanted to tell that to.

After a few more days, Susan couldn't stand it any longer, she missed Carolyn so much. Since she didn't want to be the first to say she wanted to be friends again, she called and pretended she was looking for something.

"Carolyn?" she said. "I was wondering if you had my felt hat?"

When Carolyn didn't answer right away, Susan hoped that Carolyn was going to say how much she had missed her. Then she, Susan, would come right out and say,

I missed you too! Every minute since we stopped speaking to each other, I've missed you! I never want to stop speaking to you again! And I've got a hundred million secrets to tell and no one to tell them to.

Instead
Carolyn said,
"The hat
was mine,
remember?
And you gave
it back to me."

"Oh, yes," Susan replied. "I
remember now. Carolyn . . . ?"

"Uh-huh?"

"Oh, nothing . . . I'm sorry I
bothered you."

"That's all right," said Carolyn. "It
was no bother, really."

And they hung up.

Susan felt awful. Carolyn didn't seem to care whether they would ever be friends again. But Carolyn felt just as bad. What good was a stupid old hat, she wondered, if you didn't have a best friend to lend it to?

Meanwhile, Susan had decided that she liked Carolyn more than she was mad at her. It was time for them to become friends again, if Carolyn still wanted to. Susan hoped she did. Someone had to make the first move, and she decided she would do it. Carolyn had always loved her green earrings, and they looked so good on her. So Susan wrapped them up and told her mother that she was going out.

But when she got to Carolyn's
house, Carolyn wasn't home.

"It's so nice to see you again,
Susan," Carolyn's mother said. "But
I'm afraid Carolyn went out just a
little while ago."

Susan was heartbroken. She was sure that Carolyn was on her way to see Vivian or Krishna, or whoever was her new best friend. She remembered how it had been when she and Carolyn had been best friends and they had practically lived at each other's houses. Carolyn already had a

best friend, while she, Susan, had been moping around and missing her like crazy. She felt like throwing the earrings away.

All the way home, she noticed the people in the streets. Every one of them seemed to have a best friend. Every one of them was talking and laughing together, the way really good friends do. Only she, Susan, was alone!

Then suddenly she saw Carolyn coming toward her, looking sad. As they drew closer to each other, Susan could see that Carolyn had been crying.

"What's the matter, Carolyn?" she asked, filled with sadness for her even if Carolyn did have a best friend.

"I went to your house," Carolyn answered. "But your mother said that you had gone out, and I figured you were going to Jenny's, or Emily's. I couldn't stand to think of you having another best friend!"

"Well, I did go over to my best friend's house," Susan said. "To give this to you." She handed Carolyn the package.

"What is it?" Carolyn asked.

"You'll see," Susan said shyly.

"And I went over to my best friend's house," Carolyn said. "To give this to you." She handed Susan her package.

"What is it?" asked Susan.

"It's something I think you're going to like," Carolyn said with a smile.

"Oh," Susan said when she unwrapped the package and saw the felt hat. Then she looked up and saw the way Carolyn's face lit up, which she had always liked even more than the hat.

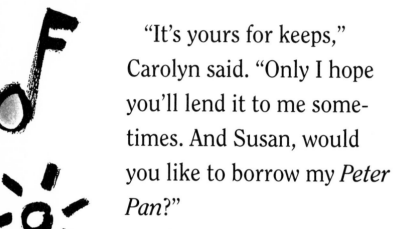

"It's yours for keeps," Carolyn said. "Only I hope you'll lend it to me sometimes. And Susan, would you like to borrow my *Peter Pan*?"

"Oh, yes! And would you like to borrow my *Wind in the Willows*?"

"Yes, and would you like to borrow my jacks?"

"Oh, yes! And would you like to borrow my orange Frisbee?"

"Yes, and would you like to borrow my polka-dot shirt?"

But underneath all of this what each of them was thinking was, *Oh, I'm so glad that we're best friends again, and I hope we always, always will be!*